W9-BYN-590

TBH, This May Be TMI

Also by Lisa Greenwald

11 Before 12
TBH, This Is So Awkward

TBH, This May Be TMI

KATHERINE TEGEN BOOKS
An Imprint of HarperCollins Publishers

LISA GREENWALD

Katherine Tegen Books is an imprint of HarperCollins Publishers.

TBH #2: TBH, This May Be TMI
Copyright © 2018 by Lisa Greenwald
Emoji icons provided by EmojiOne
Photo on page 221 © 2018 Prostock-studio/Shutterstock

Library of Congress Cataloging-in-Publication Data
Names: Greenwald, Lisa, author.
Title: TBH, this may be TMI / Lisa Greenwald.
Other titles: To be honest, this may be too much information
Description: First edition. | New York : Katherine Tegen Books, an imprint of HarperCollinsPublishers, [2018] | Series: TBH ; #2 | Summary: Told entirely in text messages, emails, and notes, best friends Prianka, Gabby, and Cecily find their friendship tested by busily planning a spring fair, bullying, and boys.
Identifiers: LCCN 2017034684 | ISBN 978-0-06-268993-1 (hardback)
Subjects: | CYAC: Friendship—Fiction. | Middle schools—Fiction. | Schools—Fiction. | Bullying—Fiction. | Toleration—Fiction. | Text messages (Cell phone systems)—Fiction. | BISAC: JUVENILE FICTION / Social Issues / Adolescence. | JUVENILE FICTION / Social Issues / Bullying. | JUVENILE FICTION / Science & Technology.
Classification: LCC PZ7.G85199 Tbh 2018 | DDC [Fic]—dc23 LC record available at https://lccn.loc.gov/2017034684

Typography by Aurora Parlagreco
18 19 20 21 22   LSCC   10 9 8 7 6 5 4
❖
First Edition

For my 2016–2017 BWL sixth-grade library students

OMGGGGGGG SPRING FAIR!!!

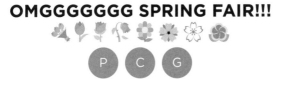

P C G

PRIANKA

Guyyyssssss, how insane is this spring fair going to be 💃🌷🌸🌼💐🌷

Soo pumped 💃😍🙌👏🎉

GABRIELLE

Can't believe it's already march & we r talking about spring fair 😱🙀😬

CECILY

Can't believe u r texting during assembly 🚫🐩

But I agree ✔️✔️

GABRIELLE

Mr. C totes just looked @ u, Pri 😳🙇

But what is this speaker even talking about 😴😴👸

Why do we need 2 know about raising chickens 🐥 🐥

PRIANKA

We r the peep squad 🐥 🐦

GABRIELLE

LOL

SILVER GIRLZZZZZZ

VICTORIA

I c u guys texting 🙀 😲 🙀

During assembly 😭 😧 😨 😬

W/o me 😭 😧 😨

Booooo 🙀 😿

LOL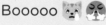

2

CECILY

Hi LOL sorry bye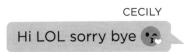

GABRIELLE

PRIANKA

V, u r funny 🙀 😹 😎 🙏 ✌️

MEMO

From: Mr. Carransey, Principal, Yorkville Middle School
To: All Middle School Students and Parents
Subject: Looking Inward; Promoting Unity

Dear students:

As you know, we had some difficulty with bullying earlier this semester. I believe we have all grown and learned a great deal about how to behave and conduct ourselves in our school community and the larger world.

We would like to continue this work. Today in each of your English classes, you will be receiving a journal where you will write down some thoughts—about how you see yourselves as individuals and how you see yourselves fitting into the larger community. We ask that you share them with peers and teachers if you are comfortable.

We will expand on this throughout the rest of the school year.

Edward Carransey
Principal
Yorkville Middle School

Be the change you want to see in the world. —Gandhi

Cecily, Mara

MARA

Cece, r u so excited 4 spring fair 👏 💐

I remember when my bro went & I was so jealous

Can we run a booth 2gether 👯 🧜 🧜

Cecily, Mara

CECILY

Hi so sorry just saw these texts

I am so excited... Not sure what 2 do bout booth but will let u know 👍

I gtg have din let's hang soon xoxo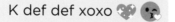

MARA

K def def xoxo 💔 😘

LUVVIIIEEESSSS 💕 💕 💕 💕 💕 💕

P   C   G

GABRIELLE

Omg u guys 🙊 🙀 😨

Did u hear what happened 🙀 👂

PRIANKA

Ummmmm

CECILY

IDK what u r talking about 🙁 🙁

GABRIELLE

Vivian Reese was caught kissing Jeremy
Cavanaugh's locker!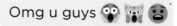

6

Ewwwwww whyyyyyy 😾 😾 🙀 😼 😼 🙀

Umm that's weird 🙀 🙀 😼 😽 🙀

Yeah and she put a letter in too w/ kiss marks all over it 😘 💋 😻 💌

Mr. Akiyama caught her doing it 😲 🙀

& TBH this may be TMI but she was so embarrassed she threw up right in the hallway 🤮 😷 😷

& she ate the sloppy joes 4 lunch 🤢 😫

OMG def TMI 😾 😹

LOL 😹

This is so awk

I barely know Vivian

Why do I need 2 know about this weirdness w/ Jeremy

Or his locker LOL or throw up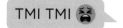

TMI TMI 😫

GABRIELLE

LOL ok ☑

PRIANKA

This is sooooooooooooooo funny 😂 🙀 🙌 👏 🎉 😂 😄 🙊 🐵 💩

Love u guyzzzzzzz 💗 💕 💞 💔 🤍 💝 💘 💖 🤍 😻 💗 💌 💗 💗

555-55

YORKVILLE MIDDLE SCHOOL TEXT/
EMAIL ALERT: We have implemented a
new text/email alert system. Keep an eye
out for important updates (not during
school hours, of course). #YorkvilleUnited

From: Douglas Katz
To: Gabrielle Katz
Subject: Summer in Austin!

Dear Gabs,

I'm going to Austin for much of the summer,
and I would love to take you with me. My
company is building a huge apartment
complex out there and it's going to have a
pool with a water slide!

I've already discussed it with Mom and she
says it's okay. But there is one potential
problem—I know you love summer in

Yorkville with your friends... so think about it and get back to me.

Love,
Dad

- -

First Journal Assignment

Please take some time to collect your thoughts about this school-wide initiative.

Before you write, ask yourself these questions:

Why is this project important?
What can I add to it?
What does tolerance mean to me?

Good luck!

SUMMER PLANSSSSSSSSSSSS

CECILY

U guys, what is every1 doing this summer ⁉️😎☀️👣

My mom keeps nagging me about deciding 😫

But IDK what 2 do 🙀🙀

PRIANKA

IK! my mom 2 😎☀️👙🕶☀️🍉

She wants us 2 go 2 India & stay w/ my cousins all summer

I wld be soooo bored w/o u guys 👯👯🙀 😑😐😔😒

And I always have to be on my best behavior there 🙄🙄🙄🙄🙄😇👳😇

11

😇 😊 😇

No thank u 😣 😨 😬

Help! 😫

GABRIELLE

My dad just asked me if I want 2 go w/ him 2 Austin 🙀 😣 😫

WTH 🚫 !

CECILY

Wait we can't all b apart 🙍 🙍 🙏

Who has a master plan

GABRIELLE

IDK

PRIANKA

Oooohh I have an idea! 💡

That camping thing ? ⛺ ⛺ ⛺

Ya know the one in Maine that we learned about during outdoor ed

Can we all go 2gether? 👭

CECILY

OMG I realllllly want to do that 👏

I am always so jeal when I see peeps camping pics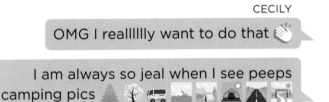

& bonus: my mom may be in2 that 2!!!!!

PRIANKA

Lets get all the deets

CECILY

K nighty night, loves

PRIANKA

ILYSM 💕 💞 🖤 💚

GABRIELLE

XOXO

Dear Journal:

I think this is a cool idea. I like that everyone in the school is doing one specific assignment.

Some kids are whining about it, saying we don't need extra work, and what's the point and all of that. But so far, I think it's cool.

Obviously, I already have a journal but I am happy to have another one. Don't get jealous. Hee hee.

Being tolerant means cooperating with everyone even if they aren't your favorite or your best friend. Even if you don't really like someone, you can be nice to them and respectful. And it also means trying to see things from everyone's point of view.

I think I can bring an open mind to the project.

Love,
Gabby

Vishal, Prianka

VISHAL

R U going 2 India 4 the summer

PRIANKA

IDK why

VISHAL

My mom said u r going w/ ur fam

She wants us to go 2

PRIANKA

Our moms are bffs now LOL
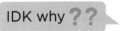

But IDK if I want 2 go

VISHAL

Why

PRIANKA

Want 2 b w/ my friends

Also so weird to stay in some1's house for sooo long 🐺 😒 😳

I am always on edge, like I need to be perf there 💯 👌 🙄 🙄 🙄 🙄 🙄 😌 🧑 😌 🧑 😌 🧑

VISHAL

Oh

U rlly luv emojis LOL

PRIANKA

👩 👩 Gtg supposed 2 b doing hw & my mom just caught me bye

Yorkville Middle School's Spring Fair
is coming up on May 1!

We need YOU to make it the best
Spring Fair ever!

Please come to the planning meeting
next Friday after school to
share your ideas.

Go Yorkville!
Mr. Akiyama, Vice Principal

SILVER GIRLS

P C G V

VICTORIA

Guys, r u going 2 the meeting 4 spring fair?

CECILY

Yesssssssss

PRIANKA

Same

GABRIELLE

Samey samey

From: Gabrielle Katz
To: Cecily Anderson, Prianka Basak
Subject: SUMMER CAMPING TRIP WOOOO HOOOO

Guys, let's have a meeting with our moms to discuss the summer plans. It'll be great. I think I'd rather spend the summer with you guys than with my dad. I see him every other night now and we have fun, but you guys are more fun. Don't tell him. LOL. 😀 😆 😆

OK, let's discuss!

XOX ILYSM
Gabs

Vishal, Prianka

VISHAL

Yo

PRIANKA

Yo yo

VISHAL

Yo yo yo

PRIANKA

Ok 🚦 🚦 🕐

What up

VISHAL

Actually it is kind of serious—

• • •

u know my cousin Arjun who lives in fla

He keeps getting bullied

PRIANKA

WDYM

VISHAL

Like bullied bc peeps r saying he is muslim

He's hindu btw

But WTH - bullied bc of religion

How messed up

PRIANKA

So awful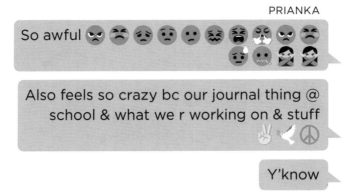

Also feels so crazy bc our journal thing @ school & what we r working on & stuff

Y'know

VISHAL

Yeah

I just feel so bad

PRIANKA

Me 2

I want 2 help

LUVVIIIEEESSSS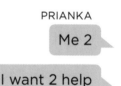

P C G

PRIANKA

I need 2 talk 2 u guys
😕 😣 👮 👮 🚑 🚒 🚨 🚓

Vishal is really upset for once

Like actually taking something seriously 😨
😬 🙀

CECILY

GABRIELLE

Sad again about no taco bar at lunch 😂😂😂😂

PRIANKA

No 4 real 🎧🎧

His cousin is getting bullied in fla

They think he is muslim (he's hindu btw) but obv no1 should be bullied for religion n e way

CECILY

Or bullied 4 anything else duh

GABRIELLE

Yeah

What can we do

PRIANKA

IDK

They just assume his religion like based on what he looks like

I just feel so bad

GABRIELLE

Me 2

CECILY

WE NEED TO COME UP WITH A TASK FORCE TO HELP WITH THIS 😡 💪

IDK what we can do from so far away but we will think of something

PRIANKA

Brb

Vishal, Prianka

PRIANKA

We need 2 help ur cousin

VISHAL

IK

PRIANKA

No 4 real

Peeps can't just get away w/ bullying some1 4 religion

& not even knowing what religion some1 is

Like not even taking time to find out & learn

I am going 2 think of something we can do

VISHAL

Thank u

VISHAL

IDK y people r like this

PRIANKA

Me neither

I'm so sorry

TASK FORCE

PRIANKA

Have u guys thought of any ideas

GABRIELLE

It's been like 5 min 😂

CECILY

Still thinking 🤚🤚

PRIANKA

U guys, I need ur help

Cecily, Gabrielle

GABRIELLE

Cece, Pri is obv so upset

She's barely using emojis

CECILY

LOL but u r right

GABRIELLE

😮‍💨😳😦😣😫😩💧💧

From: Prianka Basak
To: Evelyn Brickfeld
Subject: Guidance Appointment

Dear Ms. Brickfeld:

I wondered if I can set a time to come in and talk to you. I have a study hall seventh period. Let me know if you are ever free at that time. I can also bring my lunch to your office during lunch. (If you don't mind.)

Thank you,
Prianka Basak

Gabs, I am skipping study hall to go talk to Ms. Brickfeld. Also, can I borrow your red cardigan tomorrow? LOVE YOU BEYOND. xo Pri

HALL PASS

Prianka Basak has permission to leave study hall and speak to Ms. Brickfeld in the guidance office.

Mr. Surrey

Prianka, Cecily, Gabrielle, Victoria

GABRIELLE

Omg

We can use our comps in English now 4 in-class essays

I can totes iMessage u guys in class!!!!!!!! 👊

Any1 getting these texts

Hi Journal:

I really hope this initiative helps people. I already think I am tolerant and understanding. And I haven't had any problems with bullying here or anywhere.

But I am worried about Vishal's cousin who is being bullied based on what he looks like and what people think his religion is.

Maybe if his school had a program like this, it wouldn't have happened.

I hope we can work together to stop this craziness.

Peace on earth!

Love & Hugs,
Prianka Basak,
the extraordinary

Prianka, Cecily, Gabrielle, Victoria

PRIANKA

Gabs! I forgot 2 turn my fone off and ur iMessage came thru during the math test 😡😫😩😪🥺😶🙀

Was so loud 🚫😦😣🙀👀👀

Mrs. Silverstein was SO mad

DO NOT DO THAT AGAIN

GABRIELLE

Sorrrryyyyyyy

Using comp in study hall now

Y r u texting in guidance? 📱📱

PRIANKA

Waiting 2 go in 💆‍♀️💆‍♀️

GABRIELLE

Put phone away 📱📱

U will get in trouble again 🙀🙅😲

PRIANKA

Bye 🙏😍😘

Prianka, Cecily, Gabrielle, Victoria

(P) (C) (G) (V)

VICTORIA

😍😘😍😘😍😘😍😘

Guys, just got these texts

Snuck 2 use my phone when I went 2 the bathroom 🚽🚽

Bye 😘😘

555-55

YORKVILLE MIDDLE SCHOOL TEXT/
EMAIL ALERT: Surprise! The PA is selling
pizza in the lobby. Come by and grab a
slice! #YorkvilleUnited #Pizza #Yum

From: Evelyn Brickfeld
To: Prianka Basak
Subject: Our meeting today

Dear Prianka,

I am so glad you stopped in today. I'm sorry
about what is happening to Vishal's cousin
and I'm glad you felt comfortable coming
to talk to me about it. Please come back
to talk anytime. I'm glad you feel that our
journal project is helping you express your
feelings.

Ms. Brickfeld

Yo, Gabs—did you hear today's lunch is pasta and garlic bread? i know it's your fave. —Colin

Haha, no I hadn't heard. How do you always know the lunch so early? It's only first period. —Gabs

Haha—i guess cuz i'm always hungry. Also this class is sooooo boring.

I think it's interesting—I like math. Back to paying attention. Bye

34

Vishal, Prianka

V P

PRIANKA

Yo

VISHAL

Wut up

PRIANKA

I had a meeting with guidance bc I was so
upset about what's going on w/ Arjun

Is his fam talking to peeps there bout what
is happening

VISHAL

I think so

IDK

PRIANKA

How r u

35

VISHAL

Ok

PRIANKA

U seem bummed

VISHAL

Well I really don't wanna go to India this summer either

Also just bummed for my cousin

Like shouldn't we be past this

Feels crazy

PRIANKA

IK what u mean 😭😢😱🫣😐😬

We will help

Sometimes peeps r scared bout what they don't know 😫😫

VISHAL

Yeah 🙏

PRIANKA

Well we can make sure it doesn't happen here

& try to embrace all our differences

Like w/ the journal thingy

@ 1st I thought it was kinda dumb

But now I kinda like it

VISHAL

Yeah

PRIANKA

We can commit 2 being a tolerant place

VISHAL

Def

What is wrong with the world?

Why are people so cruel
Angry and mad and intolerant?
Why is it hard to be different?
What would it be like if we were all the same?
I can't even imagine it.
I don't think I want to.

—Prianka Basak

LUVVIIIEEESSSS

GABRIELLE

U guys - my dad is still bugging me about
Austin 😭😳😮😱

IDK what 2 do 😫😫😫

PRIANKA

U def don't want 2 go ❓❓

GABRIELLE

No 🚫

My dad is cool but all summer alone w/ him & no friends would be way awk 🚫🙅🙅🙅🐺

+ I want 2 b w/ u guys 👯👭👭

But TBH I am a bit scared 2 b away from home 🏡🏠

CECILY

Ok 1st don't stress about that bc u will b w/ us 👭🧜

2nd IDEK if my parents will agree 2 it

They r never into us leaving home + they r sooooooo overprotective 😓😭

Remember when we went 2 the movies alone 1st time last yr & we caught them sitting in the lobby when I went out 2 pee 🚽🚽

GABRIELLE

LOL that was ridic 😹😹

PRIANKA

Totes ridic 😹🙁😹👎

CECILY

😠😠

PRIANKA

We need 2 get our moms 2gether 👧👧

If 1 agrees then all will agree 👍👌👭🏆💯🙌👏🎉

GABRIELLE

But I am nervous

What if I am so homesick?

PRIANKA

I think u will totes b fine 👍👍👊👏👭👭

40

CECILY

Me 2 👍

Pos I will host a brunch this wknd for us & moms 🍩 🍵 🍳

PRIANKA

OMG amazing idea 💡💡💡 😎 🐒 🐰🐰 🌺 🌸 🌼 🏵️

GABRIELLE

K 👊

PRIANKA

So pumped 😀 😁 😆 🐱 😍 😊 😎 🎈 🎁 🎀 🎊 🎉

GABRIELLE

BTW did u guys see Colin's haircut 👦 👦

He looked sooooooo cute 💑 💑 💑

CECILY

I didn't see him today

PRIANKA

Me neither 😔😖😳😟😣😫😩😦😨 😪😭😔🙀👎

Sooooo speaking of boyz...

Did u see how Vishal was playing basketball with all the boys at recess today 🏀🏀🏃🏃

He's really good at it 2 🤚👐🙌👏🙏👍 👊✊✊✌️

CECILY

No didn't notice

GABRIELLE

I did 👏👏

They get so sweaty even though it was cold out

Why r boys so sweaty 😕

PRIANKA

LOL IDK 😆

42

GABRIELLE

Still cute when sweaty tho 😊

PRIANKA

What happened w/ Vivian Reese 😻 🎱 💋 👫 😿 😚 😗 😙

GABRIELLE

IDK haven't heard anything else

PRIANKA

Me neither

GABRIELLE

Cece ❓

PRIANKA

I think she left us 😿

GABRIELLE

LOL

I gtg 2 💚

PRIANKA

Smooches 😘 😻 💋 😍

Dear Diary,

I have neglected you because of my school journal.
I am sorry.

I feel like my head is spinning lately. I never
know what I want to do. Like, my dad wants
me to go with him to Austin this summer. But my
friends want to do a camping trip. I also feel kind
of bad leaving my mom all summer. And I'm scared
to go away from home, but I was kind of the one
in charge of starting the idea for the trip. Why
did I do that??

And then there's Colin. He always stays home
for the summer. What if we could hang out a lot
at the pool and stuff? Maybe we could really get
together. Like a real couple. I love him so much.
And he talks to me a lot more now.

How do I decide what to do? HELP!!!

Love,

Gabby

From: Cecily Anderson
To: Mama Anderson, Prianka Basak, Manjula Basak, Gabrielle Katz, Diana Katz
Subject: BRUNCH AT CHEZ ANDERSON SATURDAY

Hi moms and BFFs,

Mama Anderson and I are hosting a brunch Saturday to discuss summer plans. Be there or be square! LOL. 11am. We will have bagels and lox and muffins and fresh-squeezed OJ.

How can you say no to all that?

You can't.

XOXO Cecily Anderson

I'm not afraid of storms, for I'm learning how to sail my ship. —Louisa May Alcott

Gabrielle, Victoria

VICTORIA

Gabs, u there ❓

GABRIELLE

Yea

VICTORIA

What's up ❓

Did u think of any booth ideas 4 spring fair

I want 2 do something w/ u guys 🙌🙌

GABRIELLE

Still brainstorming 💡

Sit w/ us @ lunch tomorrow & we can discuss 🍗🍗🍕🍕

VICTORIA

Ok yay 👏❗💪👊

GABRIELLE

What r u doing 4 summer ☀️ 😎

VICTORIA

IDK pos going back 2 Philly 4 a bit

??

GABRIELLE

I am trying 2 fig out plans

Cece & Pri want 2 do this camping trip but TBH I am scared 2 go away from home 🏠🏡

I kinda told my friends that but not rlly 😭😨

I don't think they get it 😕

VICTORIA

Hmmm 👂

• • •

47

Any advice 4 me 😫

VICTORIA

Will think ⚖️

Don't fret my 🐩 🐈‍⬛ 🐰 🐟

LOL what

VICTORIA

Don't fret, my pet

I heard it once 😊

LOL OK 👍👍

From: Diana Katz
To: Manjula Basak, Elizabeth Anderson
Subject: Brunch?

Ladies,

What are our dear daughters plotting? Should I be worried?

X Diana

VNK BFF4E

VICTORIA

Guys, I feel like I am finally doing ok here 🧜‍♀️😎😍

I sat w/ those girls @ lunch today and it was soooooo much fun 👭👭👭

We text & stuff & it feels normal

I still miss u guys tho 🥹

Any1 there? 🦻 🦻

KIMBERLY

Hiiiii 🍉

We miss you 2 😫

We r trying to find a wknd 2 come visit u 🙌 🙌

NICOLE

Yesssss 👍 👍 👍 👍

Working on it 📅 📅

VICTORIA

K cool 👏 👏

KIMBERLY

Come back & spend summer in Philly 😎
😎 😎 😎 😎 😎

NICOLE

Yes do it 🔻🔻

VICTORIA

IT MAY WORK OUT 😘 😘 😘

MORE ON THAT LATER 😘 😘

KIMBERLY

Bye 🖐️ 🖐️ 🖐️ 🖐️ 🖐️

NICOLE

Tata 😘 😘 😘 😘 😘 😘

From: Cecily Anderson
To: 6th Grade Students
Subject: SPRING FAIR!!!!!!

Dear classmates:

Thanks to everyone who came to the planning meeting today, and for those of you who could not attend, there is still time to get involved!

In case you don't know, here is some information about Spring Fair!

First of all, Spring Fair is one of Yorkville Middle School's most cherished events. It's a chance to celebrate a successful year, raise money for our wonderful school and local charities, and have tons of fun together.

Yorkville students are in charge of creating and picking the booths, and each grade will be able to add 5 booths to the fair. The parents' association takes care of the big stuff like the bouncy house, the Ferris wheel, and the mega slide.

You can submit your booth ideas to me via email or write them down and give them to me in school.

I will then send a list of all the ideas to everyone, and the booths that get the most votes will be at Spring Fair.

Let me know if you have any questions.

Thank you,
Cecily Anderson, 6th grade rep

I'm not afraid of storms, for I'm learning how to sail my ship. —Louisa May Alcott

BRUNCH WITH MAMAS 👩‍👧👩‍👧👩‍👧

(P) (C) (G)

PRIANKA

On our way to Casa 🏠 Anderson 💕 💘 💖 🤍 🦝 💗 🤍 💗 💗 💞 🌍 💗 🤍

GABRIELLE

Samey samey 👍👍

CECILY

Yayyyyyyyy 👏 🐧

C u luvies soon! 💗 🐾 💜

PRIANKA

K so what is r strategy 4 this ⁉️⁉️

CECILY

We convince moms we need 2 go on camping trip & get away for a bit on our own 👏 🤜 🤛 👊 🌲

& bond w/ nature 🌲 🌴 🍀 🌿 🌱

& become independent & be all together 🏴‍☠️

PRIANKA

Yea totes 🙌 🙌 🤩 👏 🎉

Also learn about the environment 🌍 🌳

& no screens 📵 📵 which Mama Basak will 💚 🧡 🖤 ❤️

GABRIELLE

K ✓ ☑️

Got it 👍 👍 👍

BRUNCH WITH MAMAS

P C G

CECILY

OMG what are they talking about 😣 😒 😟

I know it is weird 2 text under the table but srsly WTH 😨 😬 🙀

GABRIELLE

I know 😫 💫 😮

Who is Janet?

& why r things sooooo hard 4 her ⁇ 😾 😾

CECILY

LOL 😂 😂 😂

PRIANKA

Guys, they totes know we r texting

They just did that awk mom smile @ each other 😕 😂

We need 2 get back on camping trip topic 🙏 🙏

This is verrrryyyyyy awk 😬 😫

Put phones away & start eating muffins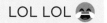

LOL LOL 😂

Vishal, Prianka

VISHAL

Yo my cousin is srsly so freaked out

He won't go to school now

His parents don't know what 2 do

He may come visit me 4 a bit

Where r u

From: Elizabeth Anderson
To: Manjula Basak, Diana Katz
Subject: Summer

Hi, ladies,

So what do we think? I'm a little apprehensive, since Cecily has never been away from home for more than a night or two, and this is three weeks! But maybe she will be okay since she will be with your girls? I should have figured this day would come; almost all of Ingrid's friends went away for the summer. And this camping trip does seem like a wonderful experience for them.

Dinner this week? I'll make a reservation at Sea Grill. Tuesday or Wednesday better?

XO E

Gabrielle, Victoria

VICTORIA

Gabs

Want 2 go 2 the movies tomw

LMK

Gabrielle, Victoria

GABRIELLE

Hi sry

I know u texted like 2 hrs ago but just saw this

I can't tomw 😨

Told my mom I'd hang w/ her 👯

Pos next wk tho 👍

VICTORIA

K no prob 😍

SUMMMERRRRRRRRRR ☀️ ☀️ ☀️

(P) (C) (G)

CECILY

Sooooo 🙍‍♀️

I think they r on board 👏 💪 💪 👊 🙌 🙌 🙏

What do u guys think 👂

PRIANKA

My mom seemed unsure on drive home 😫

She really wants this family time in India 😓
🙈 😐 😬 🙀

But I don't 🚫🚫🚫🚫🚫

It's fun there but so intense

Family together 24/7

After a few days I am so 🙄🙄🙄🙄🙄
🙄🙄🙄🙄🙄

GABRIELLE

My mom is excited about it 🧜

She thinks it will be fun

Need 2 tell my dad tho 🐨

CECILY

Well absolute last day to sign up is 4/1

So we need 2 decide soon 🙏

Think of the campfires and the hiking and
all the nature 🌳🌳🌳🌳🌳

Omg I know this is soo cheesy but

I

PRIANKA

LOL LOL

Cece's new nickname is Nature Girl

GABRIELLE

LOL

But also ack

CECILY

Why ack

GABRIELLE

IDK just feels stressful 😫

PRIANKA

IT WILL BE FABOLICIOUS

Changing topic tho

Vishal is still freaking out about his cousin
and the bullying 😪

His cousin may come here

GABRIELLE

Like move here or visit ❓❓❓❓

PRIANKA

IDK

I gtg text him back

Brb

GABRIELLE

Pri & Vish r def gonna get married 🩶

Don't u think 👫👬👫

PRIANKA

LOL

CECILY

IDK

Vishal, Prianka

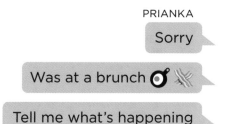

PRIANKA

Sorry

Was at a brunch 🍳 🥓

Tell me what's happening

VISHAL

His hood is just rlly racist

Peeps r soo mean 2 him

They spray painted his house

His fam may come stay w/ us for the rest of the year

And pos move here

PRIANKA

Wow

So awful

VISHAL

IK

I've never seen him like this

So messed up

PRIANKA

I want 2 help

But I gtg now

VISHAL

Peace

Dear All-Wise and Powerful Saraswathi:

Please, God, let my mom agree to the camping
trip.
I can't be the only one not allowed to go.
Please please please.
Will you even see this prayer.
I have no idea.
I hope you get it.

I love the family in India but I am almost 12
and I need to be with my friends.

Do you understand the plight of an 11-year-old
almost 12-year-old?

Thank you.
XOXO Prianka

Journal Assignment

Please take a few minutes to write down three qualities that you would use to describe yourself. Share with the person sitting to your right.

Three characteristics to describe Gabrielle Sara Katz:
1. Friendly ☺
2. Determined
3. Energetic ←‿ ←‿ ←‿

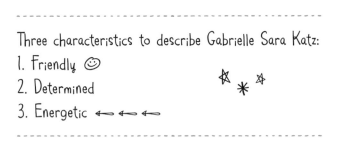

From: Douglas Katz
To: Gabrielle Katz
Subject: Summer plans

Hi Gabs,

Mom says you want to go on a camping trip this summer. That definitely sounds fun. I won't be mad if you don't come to Austin, but I do want to make a plan to do something fun the two of us this summer.

See you Thursday.

Love,
Dad

Cece, I totally forgot to do the math hw. Can u please please please help me w/ it at lunch? Wb. XO Pri

Pri, no prob. Did u bring lunch today? I did. So I won't have to wait in line. Don't worry!!!!! :) Smooches forever, Cece

Prianka Basak in three words:
1. Outgoing
2. Funny
3. Caring

Cecily Anderson's three defining characteristics:
1. Ambitious
2. Responsible
3. Thoughtful

SUMMMERRRRRRRRRR ☀ ☀ ☀

P C G

CECILY

I got the ok 4 camping trip 👊 👏 💃

Did u know we can jump from this super high rock into the lake there 🏊 🏊

& sleep under the stars 🌠 ⭐ ⭐ ⭐

And we get to cook on a real fire some days 🔥

PRIANKA

My mom is still 💯 gung ho on the India plan 😫

Will beg her 🙏 🙏

CECILY

K ☑ ✔

Let's hopefully all sign up this week 🐺🐺 🌲 🌳 🏔 🌅 ⛺ 🏕 🏕 📷 🎆

PRIANKA

K ☑ ☑

Praying 🙏 🙏

Gabs, u in ❓❓

GABRIELLE

I think so yeah

Love u 2 4ever 🖤 💕 💞 💘 🤍 🤍 💟 🩶 ❤️

CECILY

Same 😍

PRIANKA

Same 😍

Wait is it bad we r not inviting Victoria 2 come w us 🙀

CECILY

IDK

Prob not

We r nice to her but not BFF 👧👧👧👧👧👧

GABRIELLE

Agree ✔️

She said something about pos spending summer ☀️ 😎 in Philly n e way

CECILY

K good 👍

Wait we didn't discuss what happened in health 🏥

GABRIELLE

OMG I KNOOWWWWWW 😲😲😲😲

But we r not supposed 2 talk about health outside of class 🚫🚫🚫🚫

CECILY

It's just b/t us

GABRIELLE

Yeah true

PRIANKA

Ewwww IK 😦 😦 😼 😼 😔 😳

Why was Ms. T like explaining everything in such detail 👎 👎 👎 👎 👎 👎 🚫 🚫 😿 😩 🙀 😦 😬 🙀

Like w/ the periods

GABRIELLE

IK & then Vivian Reese told that story about her sister

How it all leaked out when she was sleeping 😵 😵 😵

CECILY

OMG

I am all about honesty

But I was like trying to 🙍 & say TBH this may be TMI 👖 🩲 👖

GABRIELLE

TBH that was way way way TMI
😳 😳 😳 😳 😳

PRIANKA

TBH that was beyond TMI 😬 😬 😬

CECILY

TBH now I am LOL 4 real 😹 😹

PRIANKA

Me 2

GABRIELLE

Samey samey same

3 characteristics of Victoria Melford:

1. Silly

2. Nervous

3. Hyper

Prianka, Cecily

PRIANKA

Cece, do u think Gabs is being weird about the camping trip now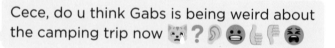

CECILY

IDK

I didn't notice

PRIANKA

K

Vishal, Prianka

VISHAL

Yo my cousin comes tonight w/ his fam ✈️ 👨🏿👩🏽👦🏿👦🏿

I thought it would be nice if I met him at the airport w/ some peeps from school

Would ur friends want 2 go 👍

PRIANKA

Um I can check

Ok to ask Victoria 2

We r trying hard to include her in stuff 👩👭👏💪💪👊👏😊

VISHAL

Cool 😎

MY GIRLZZZZZZZ

PRIANKA

U guys want 2 go meet Vishal's cousin @ the airport w/ me tonight? ✈️ ✈️ ✈️

Vishal wants peeps to go & welcome him & make him feel included after what happened ✌️ ✌️ ✌️

No pressure

But LMK 👂

VICTORIA

I can def go ✔️ ☑️

My mom can drive 2 🚗

Want her to pick everyone up?

GABRIELLE

I can't 😫 😫 😫

Dinner w/ my dad 🍔 2night

Sorry 🐨 🐨

CECILY

I'm in! 💪 💪

Thx for picking me up, V! 🚗 🚗

What time, Pri ⏰

PRIANKA

Um like 6pm?

Cool? 😎

VICTORIA

Perfect ☑️

CECILY

Same 👌

Vishal, Prianka

V P

PRIANKA

Victoria, Cece & I r gonna come w/ u 👋

Cool? 🤞🤞🤞🤞

VISHAL

Yes 👍

Fab 👏

PRIANKA

V's mom is driving us 🚗 🚗

We will meet u there

VISHAL

K - Delta arrivals terminal ✈️ ✈️

PRIANKA

K ☑️☑️☑️

MY GIRLZZZZZZZ

GABRIELLE

I am so sad I am missing this 😭😭😭

But I can't cancel on my dad

PRIANKA

It's ok

NBD

GABRIELLE

I hate to miss stuff tho 😾😾😾

Even V is going

PRIANKA

LOL 😂😂

We r being better about including her 👏
👭👱‍♀️

But don't worry - we r not replacing u!!

CECILY

Yes 💪

Proud of us 👊

GABRIELLE

I gtg

Good luck @ the airport 😘

TRUE CONFESSIONS 😖😖😖

VICTORIA

Ummmm Vishal's cousin is SO funny and cute and awesome 😍😍😍😍😍😍😍😍😍😍

PRIANKA

4 real?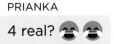

U think so?

VICTORIA

YESSSS

CECILY

LOL

We only talked to him for 5 min

VICTORIA

I could tell tho

PRIANKA

Haha ok

Go 4 it

Every1 is SO SO boy crazy

PRIANKA

Want me 2 tell Vishal u think Arjun is cute?

VICTORIA

Nooooooo 🚫🚫🚫🚫

Def not

Promise u won't????

PRIANKA

LOL 😂😂

Promise ☑ ✔

VICTORIA

Don't LOL 🤚🤚

PRIANKA

Ok

MEMO

From: Mr. Carransey, Principal, Yorkville Middle School
To: All Yorkville Middle School Students & Parents

Some of you may have heard that we received a grant from the state to purchase new laptops. They will be available for students to borrow for taking notes in class and for use in study halls and in the library.

I want to remind you and your children that these laptops are only intended for schoolwork and research. Students must treat them carefully and adhere to all the guidelines in the student handbook.

Edward Carransey
Principal
Yorkville Middle School

Be the change you want to see in the world. —Gandhi

PRIANKA

Ummmm u guysssss

U know what this means right 🐧🐧🐧🐧

We can totes iMessage in study hall now
⌨️⌨️⌨️

CECILY

No way 🚫🚫🚫🚫🚫

We will get in so much trouble 😦😦😬

I bet they will disable it somehow 🚫🚫🐱

GABRIELLE

Omg ❗❗❗❗

I can iMessage u guys all day longgggggg
🐰🐰🐰🐰

86

Dream come true 🌤️🌤️

U guys 🚫🚫🚫🚫🚫

No 🔋🔋

We r going 2 get in so much trouble & get comps taken away 🦉🦉

GABRIELLE

I can send Colin love iMessages all day long

Haha JK

CECILY

N e way - can we puhlease go back 2 discussing camping trip? 🙏🙏

GABRIELLE

BRB

PRIANKA

I gtg set the table 🍉🍉🍉🍉🍉🍉

Talk laterssss

Smooches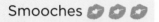

- -

Journal Assignment

Now that you have written three characteristics and discussed with a peer, please write about the experience. Did your peer agree with the characteristics? Did he or she have different ones to add? Do you feel that you see yourself in the way others see you? Please take some time to think about this and free-write in your journal.

Cecily, Mara

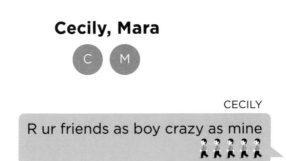

K I'm coming over 4 a bit

MARA

Arjun, Prianka

ARJUN

Prianka?

Vishal gave me ur # in case I get lost

I'm not lost LOL but I do have a ?

R we allowed to iMessage during the day?

PRIANKA

Hi

No we can't from school comps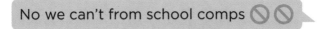

Where r u now

ARJUN

Caf

Lunch now right?

PRIANKA

Yes

Wait outside 4 me ✓ ☑

Be there soon 🏃🏃

Prianka! Arjun is so so so so cute. He made me laugh at least 6 times during lunch. Can we go bowling the 4 of us this weekend? You, me, Vishal, Arjun? Double date? Hee hee. WB. XOXO Victoria

Victoria! Don't write me notes in class. SO going to get in trouble!!!!!! Text me tonight and we can discuss. XO Pri

Dear Journal:

I sat next to Ayelet Birnbaum so we shared our characteristics with each other. She agreed about all of mine. She also said that she thinks of me as an "old soul," which is a term her grandma uses. She says I seem really grown up and mature. Maybe the most mature one in the grade. This made me sad for some reason. I don't want to seem old, especially since I still feel like a kid. Like, I am the only one who doesn't care about boys or going out with anyone. How can I seem so grown up when I feel so young?

I agreed with Ayelet's characteristics. She's really kind and empathetic and she's always thinking about other people. But she thinks of herself as shy and I was surprised to hear that. She always seems to be talking to people.

This was an interesting exercise.

—Cecily

CAMPING HERE WE COME 🦆🦆🦆

P   C   G

CECILY

U guys we r all signed up 4 camping trip 😍🐰👧😍🐰👧😍🐰👧

Did ur moms tell u

PRIANKA

Yesssssss 👏👏💪💪👊👏🙌🙏

So pumped but now that Arjun is here Vishal is staying in Yorkville 4 summer so I feel kind of bummed to miss hanging w/ them 😿😿😿

We r still going to India for 3 weeks @ the end of summer btw

CECILY

U'll have fab time w/ us 👏👏👏👏👏👏

And u can hang w/ them when we get back & b4 India

I AM SO EXCITED! 💁💁💁💁

TENT TIME w/ my BFFs 👯👯👯👯👯

GABRIELLE

LOL

PRIANKA

Gonna be awesome 😎😎😎😎

Btw do u know Victoria loves Arjun 😂😂

She wants us 2 do a double date 👩‍❤️‍👨 👫

CECILY

4 real ❓❓❓

R u going to 😼😼

PRIANKA

Maybe

I want Arjun 2 meet friends & feel comfy here

GABRIELLE

Yeah that's true 🔪 🔪

U guys should do it 😘 💋 😚

CECILY

Super awk tho - what if Arj doesn't like her like that

GABRIELLE

It's only a few hrs tho

I gtg 💚 💚 💚

CECILY

Love uuuuuuuu 💙 💙 💙

GABRIELLE

Mwah 💋 💋

PRIANKA

Tata, luvies 💙 💙 💙 💙

Dear Journal,

I didn't get to finish this in class today. I was paired up with Victoria for this week's assignment. And it was interesting to do this with her since we have had our ups and downs since she moved here.

She agrees that I am determined, especially with Colin. LOL. Why do I bring Colin into every conversation? I can't help it. (This is prob TMI for a teacher if a teacher sees this, so I'm sorry.) She also thinks I'm friendly.

When we started talking, she told me that she really wants to fit in and that she's a good listener and hardworking. I agree with all of those things, but I told her she shouldn't try that hard to fit in because she's doing okay with it.

XOXOXO Gabs

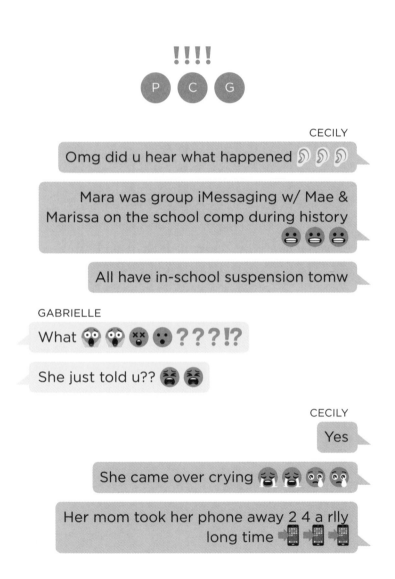

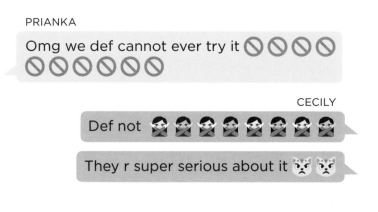

PRIANKA

Omg we def cannot ever try it 🚫🚫🚫🚫
🚫🚫🚫🚫🚫

CECILY

Def not 🥷🥷🥷🥷🥷🥷🥷🥷

They r super serious about it 😾😾

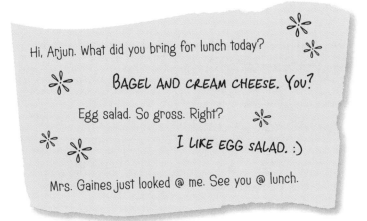

Hi, Arjun. What did you bring for lunch today?

BAGEL AND CREAM CHEESE. YOU?

Egg salad. So gross. Right?

I LIKE EGG SALAD. :)

Mrs. Gaines just looked @ me. See you @ lunch.

From: Cecily Anderson
To: 6th Grade Students
Subject: Booths for SPRING FAIR!!!!!

Thank you so much for sending in all of your booth ideas!

Here is the complete list!

Please complete the online poll with your top 5 choices.

BOOTH IDEAS:

- THROWBACK Pin the tail on the donkey
- Fortune-teller
- Guess the number of jelly beans in the jar
- Decorate a cupcake
- Oreo-eating contest
- Fastest texter contest
- Nail art
- Nerf basketball
- Marriage booth
- Magic 8 Ball booth
- Mancala competition

- Jump rope
- Photo booth
- Get the ball into the cup of whipped cream
- Pie-in-the-face game
- Knock down the bowling pins
- Dunk tank (DUNK MR. CARRANSEY)
- Spray hair dye
- Water gun through the hole of a paper plate
- Three-legged race
- Soda taste test: Coke or Pepsi
- Yorkville pizza taste test: Tomato & Company or Jennie's

Thank you,
Cecily Anderson, 6th grade rep

I'm not afraid of storms, for I'm learning how to sail my ship. —Louisa May Alcott

Dear Outdoor Explorers participants:

We are SO excited you signed up for an Outdoor Explorers camping trip this coming summer! In this packet, you'll find a packing list, a roster of your group participants, FAQs, a safety waiver for our adventure and ropes course (completely standard), and other medical forms to fill out.

Please return all paperwork with your deposit by May 15.

If you have any questions, don't hesitate to email or call!

Yours in the outdoors,

Bill Goldblatt
President, Outdoor Explorers

From: Cecily Anderson
To: 6th Grade Students
Subject: Booths for Spring Fair

Hi everyone,

Wow, you all filled out the online poll so quickly! Thank you! Here are the 6th grade booths. Each grade gets to pick five so that's why we had to narrow it down. But all of them were good ideas!

So...

1. Marriage booth
2. Magic 8 Ball booth
3. Dunk tank
4. Fastest texter
5. Decorate a cupcake

It's going to be a great fair! Come to the meeting on Friday to sign up to help out with a booth and/or bring food donations.

I also want to tell you all about Mara

Wilder's idea for an inspiring-messages wall! Everyone will have a chance to add a Post-it to the wall. So please be thinking of nice, kind, inspiring, hopeful messages!

Thank you,
Cecily Anderson, 6th grade rep

CAMPING OMG!!!!

GABRIELLE

OMG OMG OMG 💃💃💃💃💃💃💃

PRIANKA

What

GABRIELLE

The camping trip packet 📓📓📓📓

It is really happening

CECILY

So so so so so so excited 🙌🙌 🙌🙌 🙌🙌 🙌🙌

GABRIELLE

Same BUT SO SCARED NOW 😨 😨 😨

CECILY

This is my 1st time really away from home except like staying at my grandparents' house 🏡 🏡 🏡

PRIANKA

Me 2 😬

GABRIELLE

Well u guys know I went to sleepaway camp 4 a week when I was 8 and I cried the whole time 😿 😿 😿

CECILY

We r going to have the best time 👏🏻 👏🏻 👏🏻

Best 3 wks of our lives!!

OMG u guys

105

What

Every1 is obsessed w/ marriage booth 💋👦👧

Literally every1 voted 4 it

So weird

I don't get it 😾😾

Why ⁉️⁉️

I think it's cool 🏆💯👌😍🙌👏🎉💕💞💚🤍

So weird

Why r kids thinking about getting married 💖💘💝💟😻

GABRIELLE

It's just like a jokey booth, Cece 😂😂😂

No one is really getting married 😂😂😂

It's like you just walk up to the booth with a friend and have a little pretend marriage ceremony & get a certificate 👨‍👩‍👧 👰 ❤️ 💋 👩 👦 ❤️ 💋 ❤️ 👦 💍 👰

CECILY

IK

Still weird

Can't we think of other stuff that's more interesting 😒😒

Arjun, Victoria

Trying to catch up on math hw

VICTORIA

Cool 😎😎😎😎😎

IDK what

● ● ●

Dear Mara,

I know you are still without your phone, so I figured I would write you an old-fashioned letter. But I'm just putting it in your mailbox because why waste a stamp when I live next door? HAHA. Anyway, how are you? I am excited for Spring Fair. Also, do you want to try a backyard campout when it gets warmer? I'm going on a camping trip this summer and I want to prepare. Write back and answer my questions. :) XOXOXO Cecily

From: Edward Carransey
To: Priscilla Melford
Subject: Computer privileges

Dear Mrs. Melford:

Victoria was caught messaging with a peer during study hall. This is not allowed under any circumstances. She will serve an in-school suspension tomorrow in the library. Her computer privileges will be revoked for one week.

Please see me if you have any questions.

Thank you,
Edward Carransey
Principal
Yorkville Middle School

Be the change you want to see in the world.
—Gandhi

GABRIELLE

Guys, let's play a game

3 people u wld marry @ marriage booth

Ready?

PRIANKA

Vishal vishal & vishal

GABRIELLE

LOL cheater

PRIANKA

U

GABRIELLE

Colin Colin & Colin

PRIANKA

LOL LOL

GABRIELLE

Cece?

U there?

PRIANKA

Cece wld marry ummmm

Who wld Cece marry?

GABRIELLE

Well she does

PRIANKA

LOL

Cece, where r u

From: Nicole Landenor
To: Victoria Melford
Subject: WHERE ARE YOU

Vic, where are you? You haven't responded to any of my texts or emails. Are you okay? What's going on with Arjun? Please write back!!!!!! I WILL CALL YOU TONIGHT.

XOXOXOXOXOXOXOXOXO Nic

- -

Dear Journal,

This sums up how I feel rn . . .

xoxo Cecily

- -

BFFAEAEAEAEAEAEA

CECILY

Sorry I missed ur texts from b4

BUT I DON't WANT TO MARRY ANY1 🚫
🚫🚫🚫🚫 or a 🍀🌿🌱🌴🌳🌲

All u 2 think about is boys

PRIANKA

Sheesh

Calm down

Also not true

I also think about world peace 🌍🕊️🌷🌹
✌️

& Vishal's cousin & tolerance ☮️🤚🙌🙏

GABRIELLE

Same

And I spend a lot of time on our journal
assignments 📓📓📔

PRIANKA

Same

CECILY

U guys know what I mean

PRIANKA

We luv u, Cece

GABRIELLE

WLYSM

CECILY

MY GIRLZZZZZZZ

VICTORIA

U guys, I am not allowed to text or call or anything

Stole phone back from my mom's drawer just 2 text this

No time for emojis

My mom is going to email ur moms

She is very mad

Wanted 2 warn u

Bye luv u guys

GABRIELLE

Wait what

Explain more

PRIANKA

So confused

Cece, where r u?

GABRIELLE

Victoria, r u still here?

PRIANKA

WIGO

GABRIELLE

4 real

No clue

From: Priscilla Melford
To: Manjula Basak, Elizabeth Anderson, Diana Katz
Subject: Technology problems

Hello, Manjula, Elizabeth, and Diana:

I am deeply disturbed by the way our daughters communicate. Every time I look at Victoria, she is "texting" your daughters.

Victoria was "messaging" in study hall in school and her computer has been confiscated for a week.

Please speak to your children about this. I'm concerned. Victoria was never this "attached" to technology before. I am glad she has made friends, but this is unacceptable.

Thank you,
Priscilla

 **SQUAD**

P   C   G

GABRIELLE

Omg 😬😬😬😬😬

Did u hear 👂👂👂 what happened 2 Victoria

PRIANKA

That she is in loooooove with Arjun 💑👫

It's ooc 😘 ❤️ 💑👫

CECILY

Even Victoria is in luv with some1

PRIANKA

IDK

But what happened 4 real ❓❓❓❓❓❓

GABRIELLE

LOL 😂😂😂

119

U r gonna laugh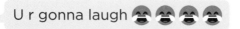

She was caught iMessaging with Arjun so now she's suspended and she lost comp privs for 1 week

CECILY

Wahhh 🙀🙀🙀

PRIANKA

That's terrible 😨😨😨😨

GABRIELLE

IK

Her mom is sooooo mad 😡😤

That's what she was warning us about

CECILY

Srsly this is why I said no iMessaging in school 4 real

PRIANKA

Totally

Guys, I am the only 1 in the grade who is not in luv w/ some1

WTH

Prianka, Gabrielle

PRIANKA

Why is Cece being so weird

I feel like she's on some kind of power trip bc she is in charge of the booths 4 spring fair & bc she is class rep & always @ meetings

GABRIELLE

Pri, that's so rude

ALSO NO SIDE CHATS

PRIANKA

Just sayin

She's also so weird about boy stuff

Did u ever realize that

Why is she scared of boys

GABRIELLE

Stop

She is who she is

Remember tolerance ✌️ ✌️ ✌️ ✌️ ✌️

& accepting each other

PRIANKA

IK but still

Victoria— r u ok? XOXO Gabs

:(not really. My parents are so so mad at me. I may never get my phone back or be able to use the computer. Crying. XOX Victoria

Hang in there. It'll be okay.

Thanks. U r a good friend.

Vishal, Prianka

VISHAL

Yo

PRIANKA

Yo yo yo

VISHAL

R u free 2 go 2 the movies w/ Arjun & Victoria this wknd

PRIANKA

Ummm 🫨 🫨

VISHAL

IDK what that means

PRIANKA

I'm thinking bout it

I thought she was in soooo much trouble

VISHAL

IDK

Arjun just asked me

PRIANKA

Ok I'll go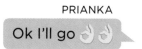

VISHAL

Cool

Bye

Hi Hi Best Neighbor Ever Dear Cecily,
I had so much fun hanging with you yesterday.
I am so sorry I lost your other letter and never
wrote back. Please forgive me. We will def do
that backyard camping trip.

But I forgot to ask and I need to know who first
suggested marriage booth. Now everyone is
obsessed with it. I am so curious. I don't get it.
And I kind of hate how all the girls are so boy
crazy. There is more to life than talking about
boys! Ya know?!!?

Also, so so happy you love my "inspiring-messages
wall" at the fair! It will look so cool when
we have little pieces of colorful paper all over
covered with happy, inspiring things on them.

I didn't even realize this when I first thought of
it but it goes with the theme this semester of
looking inward and exploring our diversity or

whatever it's called.

What do you think of my calligraphy? Just started a calligraphy class at the community center.

Cool calligraphy, right? ⁵
    Want to come over for pizza Friday?
    XOXO Mara

Hi Mara—
Nice calligraphy. Impressed!
    I can't tell you who suggested it, I have to keep all ideas anonymous. But yeah, everyone is obsessed. So weird.
    I am so glad you feel the same way I do about all the boy craziness. There is so much more to talk and think about. The boys in our grade are soooo immature.
    Yes pizza this Friday!!!!!!!!!!!
    XOXO Cecily

Dear Diary,

I haven't written in you in soooo long. TBH, I kind of forgot about you. So sorry! I know that's really mean. Things are good though. I'm going on a camping trip with Cecily and Prianka this summer. But I am so so nervous about it. I don't even know if I like that naturey adventure stuff. I pretty much hate hiking. And what if I don't like the other kids? Sometimes I wonder if I will just bail last minute. Would my friends hate me? I still love Colin. Just in case you were wondering. :)

Anyway, that's all for now. Bye!

XOXO
Gabby

Arjun, Victoria

A V

VICTORIA

Finally got my phone back

How r u

ARJUN

Ok

VICTORIA

What's wrong

ARJUN

Peeps from my old school r still bugging me

They r emailing me all this rude stuff & texting me

My mom may have to call the police

So messed up

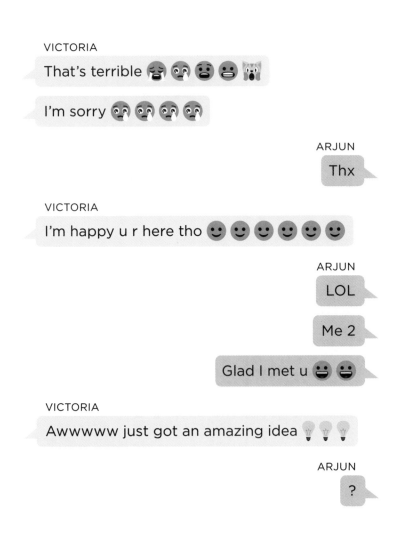

VICTORIA

U should make a speech at an assembly one day soon

Abt what happened to u & how we can't let it happen here ✌️✌️✌️✌️

Raise awareness and stuff

U know they r always asking 4 student speakers

ARJUN

4 real?

VICTORIA

Yes def 👏👏🙌🙌🙌👏🙌⛲

ARJUN

IDK

I just got here

VICTORIA

That's why its so powerful 👊👊👊👊👊

131

I was new this yr 2

And it's sooooooo hard

ARJUN

Yeah IDK

VICTORIA

Well think about it

ARJUN

K

gtg

See u tomrw

VICTORIA

Bye

132

P C G

PRIANKA

Omg I am freaking out about this double date 😱😱😱😱😱😱😱😱😱😱 😱😱😱😱😱😱😱

It suddenly feels soooo serious 😱 😱 😱 😱 😱 😱

I can't even change my emojis RN

Where r u guys 😱 😱 😱 😱 😱 😱

Answer me 😬 😬

R u 2 hanging w/o me 😫 😫 😫 😫 😫 😫

I mean honestly who would've thought my 1st double date wld be w/ Victoria?????? 🐺🐺🐺🐺🐺🐺🐺🐺

Hellooooooooooooo 👂 👂 👂 👂 👂

 **SQUAD**

P   C   G

CECILY

So sorry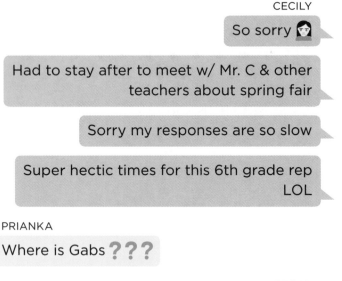

Had to stay after to meet w/ Mr. C & other teachers about spring fair

Sorry my responses are so slow

Super hectic times for this 6th grade rep LOL

PRIANKA

Where is Gabs ❓❓❓

CECILY

IDK

PRIANKA

So weird

So what should I do about this double date 😐 😐 😫

Do I sit b/t Vish and Arj @ the movie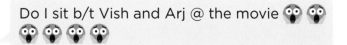

CECILY

IDK

U know I have no idea about any of this stuff

I can ask Ingrid b/c she has some boy experience

PRIANKA

Nooooooo

CECILY

LOL 😂 😂 😂

OK

So just go w/ it 💕 💕

It'll be ok

PRIANKA

Fine whatever

GABRIELLE

Hiiii, guys 👋🏻 👋🏻 👋🏻

Sorry I am chiming in so late

U r never going to believe this

Ready ???????

CECILY

Ummmm scared but ok 😬 😬

PRIANKA

Same 😬 😬

GABRIELLE

Sooooo... Colin came up to me @ the bus 🚌 🚌 🚌 line

And he sat next to m

me

& then he asked if he could walk me home 🏠 🏠 🏠

PRIANKA

WHATTTTTTTTTTTT 🐺🐺🐺🐺

CECILY

GO ON 👂👂👂

GABRIELLE

So I said ok

My mom was gonna be home 🏡🏡🏡 though sooooo awk

And he came over for like 15 min

CECILY

Wowie

GABRIELLE

WAIT

We walked outside when he was leaving

AND HE KISSED ME RIGHT THERE BY THE SIDE OF MY HOUSE OMGGGGGGGGGGGGGGGG 😘😘😘😘 😘😘😘😘😘😘

PRIANKA

Whattttt

GABRIELLE

I KNOW 🙀🙀

I was not ready

I mean I was bc I've liked him 4ever
🖤🖤🖤

But I didn't expect that AT ALL

CECILY

U had ur 1st kiss today 😱😱😱

TBH THIS IS A BIG DEAL 😱😱😱

And u told us over text 😱😱😱

OMGGGGGGGGGG 😱😱😱

GABRIELLE

I knoooowwwww 😍😍😍😍

138

What does this mean ‼️❓❓‼️❓❓

PRIANKA

Ummmmm

He obv likes u 🖤💕🌍💟🤍🤍🌎💓🖤

GABRIELLE

Yeah

But I mean do we hang out again ‼️⁉️

Do we kiss all the time now 😘💋😘💋

CECILY

LOL 😂😂

Not in school 🏫🎒🏫🎒

PRIANKA

Def not 🚫🚫

This is sooooo weirddddd 👽👻👽👻👽👻

GABRIELLE

Bugging out

CECILY

I gtg help my mom bring in groceries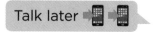

Talk later 📱 📱

PRIANKA

I want more deets, Gabs

Pleaaaaaseeeeeeeeeee

GABRIELLE

That's really itttttttt

But srsly buggin

PRIANKA

K I gtg 2 Xoxoxo

GABRIELLE

Bye, loves 💜 💜 🤍 🤍

Cecily, Mara

CECILY

U there

I have 2 tell u something

Promise u won't tell

MARA

Hi yea

CECILY

Gabby had her 1st kiss 2day

Isn't that so crazy

MARA

OMG yes

CECILY

I have never liked any1

have u

MARA

Noooooo 😐 😐 😐

CECILY

K 🙂 😃 😃

MARA

LOL 👊

Dear Cece,
I kind of like how we write each other
real letters, don't you? Anyway, you are
the best neighbor in the world. You're an
amazing 6th grade rep, and an all-around
wonderful person! Don't stress about the
boy stuff. You rock. XOXOX Mara

Vishal, Prianka

VISHAL

Yo

PRIANKA

Yo yo

VISHAL

R u & Victoria meeting us @ movies

PRIANKA

Ummm IDK

I guess so

VISHAL

K see u there at 4:30

We need time 2 get snacks

PRIANKA

K ✓

143

Victoria, Prianka

PRIANKA

Can ur mom drive 🚗🚗🚗🚗🚗🚗 us 2 the movies

My mom has to take my bro to soccer ⚽⚽⚽⚽⚽

And my dad is out of town

VICTORIA

Sure 👍👍

R we meeting Vishal & Arjie there

PRIANKA

Yes 👍

VICTORIA

K don't say anything about Arjie and Vishal coming

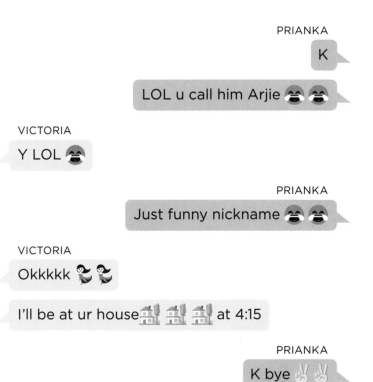

PRIANKA

K

LOL u call him Arjie 😂 😂

VICTORIA

Y LOL 😂

PRIANKA

Just funny nickname 😂 😂

VICTORIA

Okkkkk 👧 👧

I'll be at ur house 🏡 🏡 🏡 at 4:15

PRIANKA

K bye ✌️ ✌️

145

P **C** **G**

CECILY

R u at the movies 🎬🎬🎬

Bugging out 4 u 😲😲😲

Need all deets

PRIANKA

We r here 🎬🎬

In line 4 snacks 🍿🍿🍿🍿🍿🍿

Victoria has her arm around Arjun LOL 😂😂

I think he is soooo confused 😂😂😂😂

CECILY

Y confused?

146

PRIANKA

Bc Victoria like scooped him up 😘💋😗

IDK I can't explain it

CECILY

Ok well good luck ✌️✌️✌️✌️

I want all deets when u get home

PRIANKA

K def 👍👍

CECILY

Promise 🙏 🙏

PRIANKA

Of course bye xoxoxoxo 🤍💟🖤💜🤍
💟🖤💜

CECILY

Xoxoxoxo

Unknown, Cecily

MAYBE: CAMILA

Hi, Cecily, this is ur # rite

It's Camila from English

I want to bring food in for the fair

My dad makes amazing tamales

Sorry if this is 2 late 2 text u

Camila, Cecily

From: Colin Hayes
To: Cecily Anderson
Subject: Idea

Hi,

Remember when we were badminton partners? LOL.

But for real I had an idea. I think some money raised from Spring Fair should be donated to refugee families. Ya know how it's so hard for them to even come here? And then get resettled? A refugee family moved in with some peeps around the corner from me and I know they would love to get their own place but it is so hard. They also have like 5 kids.

There are so many families like that I bet.

Anyway, just an idea.

Peace,
Colin

Dear Diary,

Is that what I will call you? I wonder if I will ever really write in you. No offense. But I'm not really a diary person. We also have a journal for school now and it's sort of gotten me into the idea of writing down my thoughts but I'm glad to have a private one.

Aunt Sheila brought you to me when she came to stay last summer and I just saw you sitting on my shelf looking so lonely and I have a lot on my mind so I figured I'd write in you.

Anyway... I can't fall asleep.

Not much going on. Well, that's not true. Colin kissed Gabby. And Prianka is on a double date right now. So I guess I feel kind of left out in that area. And everyone is obsessed with this marriage booth thing at Spring Fair. But I don't really like anyone. At least I don't think I do. I mean, Kenny Fong is kind of cute but we don't really talk except for when he asks me what the math homework is. At least Mara doesn't like anyone either. That makes me feel better. She's lived next door my whole life but we only became friends this year. So weird.

Also it's weird that everyone is so excited about a marriage booth at the fair. Like why can't we just be kids for a little longer? It feels like everyone is in such a rush to be grown up and I don't get it. I like being a kid.

Any advice?

LOL. I didn't think so.

Well, see ya soon.

Love,

Cecily

 **UPDATE**

P C G

PRIANKA

I just snuck out to the bathroom

Gotta make this quick

Vishal put his arm around me in the movie for 13 seconds 😲 😲 😲

I counted but then he took it away

What does this mean ❔ ❔ ❔

GABRIELLE

LOL 😂 😂 No clue

R u having fun tho

PRIANKA

Uh I think so 💁 💁 💁 💁 💁 💁

IDK

R Victoria and Arjun all cuddly

PRIANKA

Kinda but not too much

They r sharing popcorn 🍿🍿🍿

CECILY

Wowwwie

PRIANKA

What if Vishal wants 2 hold my hand or something 4 the rest of the movie

GABRIELLE

U can always say ur hands r sweaty

PRIANKA

K good idea

GABRIELLE

Go back 2 the movie, Pri 💕💞

U r doing great

PRIANKA

K bye

Colin, Gabrielle

COLIN

Yo

GABRIELLE

Hi hi

COLIN

I hope that wasn't weird the other day

IDK what happened

GABRIELLE

Um it wasn't that weird

COLIN

Ok good

GABRIELLE

So what else is up

COLIN

Nothin

Playin video games

GABRIELLE

Cool

COLIN

U

GABRIELLE

NM

Excited 4 spring fair

R u

COLIN

Yeah

GABRIELLE

Cool

COLIN

Cool

Dear Journal,

OMG I can't even write what happened because my mom snoops. (HI, MOM! STOP SNOOPING! NOW! I KNOW YOU'RE STILL READING! STOP!)

Anyway, something major happened. That's all. Bye! Love you!

—Gabby

From: Cecily Anderson
To: Colin Hayes
Subject: RE: Idea

Hi Colin,

Lol badminton!

That is a great idea. Sorry I am so slow to reply. Life is so hectic being 6th grade rep. It's more meetings than people realize! And I am already starting to plan Spirit Week! Wait for that in June... :)

I will make sure some of the money we raise goes to refugee families settling in Yorkville.

Bye!
Cecily

I'm not afraid of storms, for I'm learning how to sail my ship. —Louisa May Alcott

CPG4EVA

(P) (C) (G)

PRIANKA

U guys r never going to believe this 😲😲😲

R u there 👂👂👂

Helllooooo ⁉️⁉️⁉️⁉️⁉️⁉️

CECILY

Hi sorry 👋👋

PRIANKA

Gabs ❓❓

GABRIELLE

Hi here 2 👋👋👋👋

Sorry 😗😗

What happened ❓❓

PRIANKA

Ready ??

CECILY

Yes just tell us 🙌🙏🙌🙏🙌🙏

PRIANKA

K so at the end of the movie we were waiting for our rides and we were all just standing around and then Victoria goes to Arjun "I know this is gonna be weird but I wondered if we could, like, go out?" 😂😂

And then Arjun was like "but we are out right now" 🤭🤭🤭🤭

And then Victoria said "I mean like as a couple" 👫👫👫

And then Arjun was like "oh, um, ok that works" 😜

LOL LOL LOL 😂😂😂😂😂😂

GABRIELLE

OMG 😲😲😲

CECILY

I KNOW

PRIANKA

It was soooo funny 😂😂

CECILY

What did Vishal say

PRIANKA

He was cracking up so much 😁😁😂😂

GABRIELLE

This is so so funny 😹😹😹😹

PRIANKA

I think Arjun is so overwhelmed

He went from major bullying in his old school and then moved and now there is a girl in love 🩶🩶 w/ him here

And did u hear he is going to speak at an assembly

About racial tolerance and stuff !!!

PRIANKA

IK ✌️👏👏

It was Victoria's idea

This is so crazy tho

GABRIELLE

I think it's good 👍👍👍

Yorkville is a nice place ✌️✌️

CECILY

Def def def 🖤🖤🖤

GABRIELLE

What's up w/ u & Vishal, Pri

PRIANKA

WDYM

GABRIELLE

IDK

R u a couple 👫👫🧍‍♀️👫👫

PRIANKA

No clue

CECILY

We don't need to all have bfs, Gabs

GABRIELLE

I know

Was just asking

Sheesh

U r obsessed with telling us what to do
about boys

I'm just saying

GABRIELLE

I don't have a bf

CECILY

But u kissed Colin

GABRIELLE

Yeah but still

PRIANKA

K I gtg, girlies 😘

See u tomw 😘 😘

CECILY

Bye

GABRIELLE

Xoxoxoxox

Prianka, Gabrielle

That was awk 😱 😱 😱

IK 😫

I AM IN LOVEEEEEEEEEE

P C G V

VICTORIA

U guys

I am in luv w/ Arjun 🖤🏵️🤍💗💟🖤🖤

4 real

& I know he came here 4 a bad reason but I kinda feel like it was meant 2 be 👫👫

PRIANKA

LOL 🐨🐨🐨🐨

Silver lining 🌥️🌥️🌥️🌥️🌥️

VICTORIA

Yeah bc we R THE SILVER GIRLS

GABRIELLE

LOL

Glad u r so happy, V! 👏🏻👏🏻👏🏻👏🏻

Journal Assignment

At lunch today, go up to a classmate you don't know very well. Ask questions about them—the first three that come to your mind. Write down the questions and the answers and how you felt about this exercise. Have fun!

WHATTTTTTTTTTTTTTTTTT

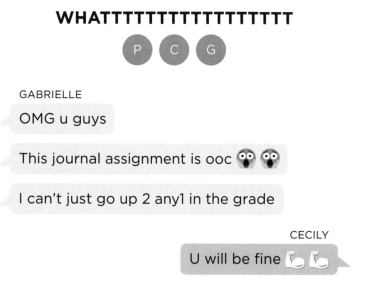

P C G

GABRIELLE

OMG u guys

This journal assignment is ooc 😲 😲

I can't just go up 2 any1 in the grade

CECILY

U will be fine 💪 💪

GABRIELLE

At 1st I was so into this journal stuff bc it was a good way to bump up my average

But now I am so 😫 😩 😨

PRIANKA

LOL it is a bit nutty

CECILY

Guys, it's not a big deal

Prianka, Gabrielle

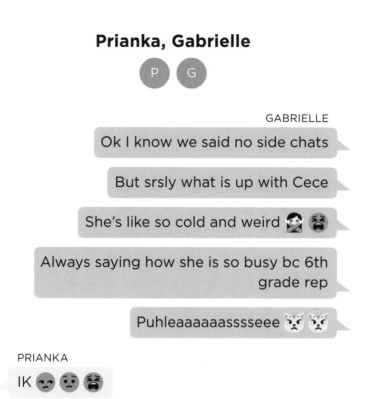

GABRIELLE

Ok I know we said no side chats

But srsly what is up with Cece

She's like so cold and weird 🙅‍♀️ 😫

Always saying how she is so busy bc 6th grade rep

Puhleaaaaaasssseee 😾 😾

PRIANKA

IK 😒 😟 😫

Maybe we need 2 speak 2 Ms. Brickfeld

GABRIELLE

Hmmm

Dear Journal,

So I went up to Sanda Yanusz at lunch today. I don't know her at all. I didn't even know her name. We weren't in the same elementary school. I just looked around the cafeteria and picked a person and said, "Hi, I'm Gabby. Can we talk for the journal assignment?" And she said, "Yes! I was so scared to go up to someone and I'm so happy you came up to me!"

We talked for ten minutes. She has two brothers and they're identical twins. Her favorite food is pizza and I also said, "What's one cool thing about you that not many people know?" She said, "I actually really like bugs! They don't scare me at all and I love to watch them. But I don't tell people because it seems so embarrassing."

I really liked this exercise. I think I will say hi to Sanda in the hallway all the time now. And hopefully she says hi to me too!

—Gabby

Arjun, Victoria

VICTORIA

Arjun, I had soooo much fun @ movies w/ u

Did u have fun 🍿 🍿

Where r u

Helllooooooo

???

Victoria, Prianka

VICTORIA

Hi, Prianka

Do u know where Arjun is ❓❓❓❓

PRIANKA

LOL 😼😼😼😼

He's here now 😎 😎

My mom had a bunch of fams over

R u jealous LOL 😼😼😼😼

VICTORIA

Grrrr 😠 😖

He didn't respond 2 my texts 😠 😖

PRIANKA

He's not looking @ his fone 😂 😂 😂

Don't worry

Gtg bye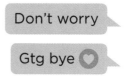

HELP ME

(V) (N) (K)

VICTORIA

U guys I need ur help !!!!

I think Arjie hates me already

NICOLE

Y

VICTORIA

He didn't respond to my texts today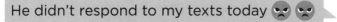

I found out where he is but still

173

KIMBERLY

Calm down, V 😼😼😼😼

He's obv busy

Of course he likes u bc u r awesome!

NICOLE

Yeah!!! 😻😻😻

VICTORIA

K deep breaths

NICOLE

LOL

VICTORIA

Bye smooches 💋💋💋

Dear Journal,

I have been so busy with Spring Fair I didn't get a chance to do this journal entry. I went up to one of the girls who sit at the back table in the cafeteria. Everyone thinks they're so popular but I don't know if they really are. I ended up talking to a girl named Phoebe McGellin. She wasn't super friendly. I asked her what she's most proud of and she said that her dance team got second place in a competition. Then I asked her what she's most scared of and she said getting struck by lightning. Then I asked her what her favorite movie is and she said she doesn't really have one.

It was an okay experience but it's hard to talk to someone you don't really know. She said she knew who I am since I'm the class rep.

I think one thing I've realized this year and especially since doing this journal is that I feel really different from everyone else. I may not look different but I just don't feel the same as the rest of my grade.

I don't know why. And maybe no one knows I feel like this. Maybe even my own friends don't know. I like being the class rep and running meetings but I feel like I am kind of on the outside looking in. I bet everyone thinks I am so confident since I am on student council. But I don't feel that way at all.

—Cecily

—Prianka

 **SQUAD**

P C G

PRIANKA

OMG!!!!!

A news team just showed up at Vishal's house 🎥🎥🎥

Apparently there r stories like Arjun's fam all over the country and they r doing a story on it 😲 😲 😲

CECILY

4 real? 🐺🐺🐺🐺

Horrible 😠 😠 😠

R U SERIOUS❓❓❓

PRIANKA

YES

Will tell u more later

Wait sorry I am slow & missed this whole thing 🐱 🐱 🐱

Scroll up xoxo

Gabby—will you marry me at the marriage booth at the fair? —Colin

Colin—I will consider it. —Gabby

Prianka, Gabrielle

P · G

GABRIELLE

Pri, u there ❓❓❓

PRIANKA

Yo 😊 😊

GABRIELLE

Colin asked me 2 marry him @ the fair ❗❗❗❗

PRIANKA

OMG 🙀 🙀 🙀 🙀

GABRIELLE

I'm not telling Cece

She will get upset

PRIANKA

Ok

Well mazel tov 👏 👏

GABRIELLE

LOL

 **SQUAD**

P   C   G

CECILY

U guys, did u see the list 4 camping trip 👏🏻👏🏻

Soooooooooo excited 💃💃💃

PRIANKA

I am soooooooooo excited but I can't forget to buy the flashlights and the shower caddy 🙌🏻🙌🏻

Vishal and Arjun are gonna be so bored w/o me 😭😭😭😭 LOL

CECILY

LOL we r going 2 have best time 😎 😎 😎

PRIANKA

Hello CAMPING PREP STARTS RIGHT NOW 😎 ⛺ 😎

GABRIELLE

Yeah about that...

PRIANKA

What ⁉❓⁉❓⁉❓

GABRIELLE

I feel like I haven't been totes honest with u guys...

I'm getting rlly nervous 😥 😫

CECILY

Gabs, it will be gr8 👍 👍

PRIANKA

Better than gr8 💃 💃 💃 💃

Uber fab ‼️‼️

GABRIELLE

Just sooooo nervous 😦😦😦

I don't really like all that nature stuff LOL
😂😂

IDK about the adventure course stuff
😵😵😵

PRIANKA

U can't bail, Gabs 😬😬

CECILY

We will be there w/ u 🐺🐺🐺

GABRIELLE

IK

I gtg talk l8r 😻

Prianka, Cecily

PRIANKA

OMG CECE

I think Gabs is gonna bail 😭 🫥 😦 😬 🙀 🙀 🙀 🙀

CECILY

Stop 🎚️ 🎚️

PRIANKA

No 4 real 😡 😣

CECILY

Stop side chatting, Pri 🚫 🚫 🚫 🚫 🚫

PRIANKA

K fine bye

Cece, this is gonna be OPERATION CONVINCE GABS SHE HAS TO GO ON THE CAMPING TRIP. I'm writing you a note since you hate side chats. We will leave a note in her mailbox every day like we did with the Yorkville ones. Okay? Write back and let me know you got this. XOXOXOXO Pri

Pri—yes, I got your note. But calm down. She's just nervous. Let's not freak out yet. She's still going. We just need to reassure her. We don't need to do the mailbox notes.

Love you, Cece

Vishal, Arjun

VISHAL

Yo

U ready for ur big speech

ARJUN

No, dude

Why am I giving a speech again 👎👎

VISHAL

LOL IDK

ARJUN

& why so soon

VISHAL

No 4 real u will be gr8 👍👍👍

ARJUN

This is wack

VISHAL

No stress, bro

U will crush it

ARJUN

LOL thank u

Peace

VISHAL

Peace, bro

Gabs, are you still nervous about the camping trip? Please don't be. We will have the best time. Also what is this sub even talking about? I have no idea. I love you! Pri

I am nervous and excited and I have no clue what he is talking about either. But I am so scared we are gonna get in trouble for passing notes, so don't write back to this one. OK? But I love you. XO Gabs

From: Arjun Gobin
To: Victoria Melford
Subject: SPEEEEEEEECH

Hi Victoria,

Will you read my speech and tell me what you think? I'm really nervous. I didn't even show this to Vishal yet. Thanks for your help.

Arjun

Speech for Assembly

Hi, everyone. Good morning. For those of you who don't know me, my name is Arjun Gobin. There are probably a lot of you who don't know me since I'm new here.

The area that I came from in Florida was really different from Yorkville. It was not a tolerant place at all. I was bullied based on what I looked like. People tormented me because of my religion even though they didn't even know my religion. No one even took the time to find out. Kids I have known forever turned against me. I was told I was not welcome there. Eggs were thrown at my home.

This all happened out of nowhere. I can't say for sure why this started happening but it somehow became a normal thing. The school board and teachers and principal tried to step in but the cruelty continued. Eventually it became so difficult to stay there that my family and I moved here and we are staying with my cousins, my dad's brother's family.

You've all been welcoming and kind to me. I've only been here a short time, but I can already tell that there are so many different types of people in Yorkville, different religions and ethnicities. It doesn't even seem like a big deal to be different here.

I wanted to tell you a little bit about what happened to me so that we are sure to never repeat it here. We need to embrace our differences and learn from one another. Sometimes I think people are scared of people who are different. So the only way to fix that is to take the time and talk to our peers and our classmates and our neighbors. Then we can work together to make our school and the world a better place.

Thanks for listening and for welcoming my family and me to Yorkville.

Have a great day.

Guys, I have the best idea. I bought this notebook at the school store. We're going to start a group packing list. I'll write a few things, then pass it to one of you, then you write a few things and pass it to the next person. We'll add stuff each day and then go shopping together or order online and we'll all have what we need. Sound good?

OOOOH I love a new notebook. Amazing idea, Pri!!! I am totally on board. We can pass it to each other between classes but let's not make it a big deal so people don't feel left out. LOVE YOU GUYS!

Yes, I love this idea too!! This is definitely making me less nervous. Okay, I'm starting the list.
1. Sunglasses
2. Sunscreen
3. Cute dresses

SQUADDDDDDDD

(P) (C) (G)

GABRIELLE

Did u guys hear that Phoebe McGellin is marrying Emilio Carbonelli at the fair ‼️‼️‼️‼️💐👰

PRIANKA

Whatttt 😲 😲

How r u even keeping track of this 😼 😼

CECILY

Yeah and why do u care ❓❓❓

GABRIELLE

CECE

U R SO RUDE

CECILY

We don't even know them 😡 😖 😡 😖

Prianka, Gabrielle

GABRIELLE
Ok now things r really weird 🐺🐺🐺

PRIANKA
IK

GABRIELLE
We r never going to make it camping 🏞️🏞️🌲🌲

PRIANKA
STOP 🔋🎧🎧

U R JUST SCARED

GABRIELLE
Well Cece is being soo rude 😭😭

PRIANKA
Calm down

From: Cecily Anderson
To: Gabrielle Katz, Prianka Basak
Subject: What is going on?

Dear Gabs and Pri,

I am just going to come right out and say this. I feel like things are really distant between us. I am not sure why. We had the drama with Victoria and we got past that. And we figured out our summer plan and I am really excited about it. I know you're nervous, Gabs, but it will be great.

But I feel like it always comes back to boys with you guys, and everyone is obsessed with this dumb marriage booth. And I just don't get it. Is it possible to still be BFF with you guys if I'm not like totally in love with a boy? Are you bored of me? Have we outgrown each other?

Love, Cece

PS: Sorry so many questions.
PPS: I really hope we can still be BFF.

Arjun, Victoria

VICTORIA

Yo Arjun

Just read ur speech

AMAAAAZZZZZIIIINNNNNGGG 💯 💯 💯 💯 💯 💯

ARJUN

Really?

R u telling the truth

VICTORIA

Yes so so so so good 👏 👏 💪 💪 👊 👏 🙌 👐

ARJUN

Ok thank u

VICTORIA

U will be so great 🙌💅🙌💅🙌💅

ARJUN

I never shoulda agreed 2 this

VICTORIA

Yes u should ✌️✌️✌️✌️✌️✌️✌️

Glad u did

ARJUN

Ok

VICTORIA

I gtg C u tomw

ARJUN

Ok bye

Prianka, Gabrielle

PRIANKA

What should we wb 2 Cece

I feel like she is so upset

GABRIELLE

Me 2

I don't want there 2 be drama b/t us

PRIANKA

Me neither

That was obvs never our intention

GABRIELLE

But why does she get so upset w/ boy stuff

PRIANKA

IDK

& I don't like how she makes us feel bad about it

GABRIELLE

Same

PRIANKA

I will wb & say we should get 2gether 2 discuss

K?

GABRIELLE

K

From: Prianka Basak
To: Cecily Anderson, Gabrielle Katz
Subject: RE: What is going on?

Dear Cece,

First of all, I am so sorry you're upset and feeling sad. Obviously Gabs and I love you so much and never wanted to make you feel that way.

Can we please all get together to talk about this? We can obvs still be BFF even if you don't like a boy. I mean, duh. It shouldn't be something that divides us.

Love, Pri

PS: No we are not growing apart.
PPS: DUH.

BACK 2 TEXTING PLEEEAAAASSEE

P   C   G

CECILY

Guys this email thing seems so formal 👩👩👩

Can we please text 📱➡️📱

I am sooo stressed about spring fair

There r like a million things 2 do 4 it

And I miss u guys so much 😔 😔 😔

GABRIELLE

Yes hi ✋ ✋ ✋ ✋

PRIANKA

Ceeeeece, don't be sad 😀 😀 😀 😀

CECILY

I just feel so awk 😬 😬 😬

Guysssss, we got off topic but I wanted to write a note in this journal so we can discuss what has been going on a bit more. Do you understand how I feel? Is it okay to go a little lighter on all the boy talk sometimes? I love you. —Cece

Yeah, I think we can do that. And can you also understand that I am 100% freaking out about the camping trip. Will they make us pee in the woods? Use leaves as toilet paper? UGGGHH. Crying. Tolerance, people. Tolerance. —Gabs

Okay, okay. We will all be tolerant of each other's weirdnesses. JK. But we are all weird. And that's the fun of it. Shouldn't that be our school slogan? Let's embrace each other's weirdnesses. Is weirdnesses even a word? LOL. I LOVE YOU 2 WEIRDOS 4ever! —Pri, the extraordinary :)

CPG4Eva

PRIANKA

GABRIELLE

CECILY

BEST DAY EVERRRRRRR

PRIANKA

Guys, this fair is going soooo well 👍👍👍👍

I've barely seen u guys

Where r u ❓❓❓

Victoria has married 3 peeps btw 💍💍💍

Thought she would only want 2 marry Arjun

But she married Kelly O'Neal too

& randomly Mae Revis & Jared Remington @ the same time LOL

Can we all marry each other puhlease

Where r uuuuuuu guyzzzzzz 😒😐😩😞
😹😼😹😺

Hiiiii

Let's all marry each other RIGHT NOW

And don't forget to post inspiring messages on the wall

U guys r soooooooo inspiring

Certificate of Marriage

On this day in
May 2018

<u>Prianka Basak and
Cecily Anderson and Gabrielle Katz</u>

were joined together in marriage
by the state of
Yorkville Middle School.

Witness: <u>Jamal P.</u>

555-55

YORKVILLE MIDDLE SCHOOL TEXT/EMAIL
ALERT: Attention all students: come to the
photo booth area! We are going to try and
get each grade together in a group photo.
Hard but not impossible! #YorkvilleUnited

Mara, Cecily

MARA

Cece, did u see the text alert

It was my idea & I told Mr. Akiyama and he
🖤 it

CECILY

OMG Yes I 🖤 it 2

On my way

YOU ARE NOT ALONE

Never give up!
You are doing
great!

You are perfect
just the way
you are.

JUST KEEP
SWIMMING.

Good Vibes
Only.

You are a
superstar.

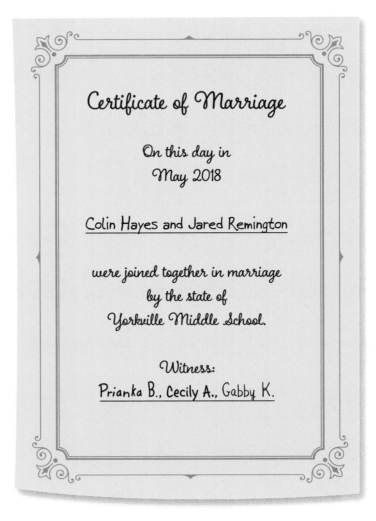

Certificate of Marriage

On this day in
May 2018

Colin Hayes and Jared Remington

were joined together in marriage
by the state of
Yorkville Middle School.

Witness:
Prianka B., Cecily A., Gabby K.

DUNK TANK NOW

P C G

CECILY

How awesome was that photo 👏👏💪💪👊🤞

Really feel like we united as a grade 👫👫👫👫👫👫😊😊😊😊😊😊

We rlly r a tolerant school, don't u think

Is that sooo cheesy 2 say

Where r u guys

Meet me at the dunk tank 💦💦🌊

They r about to dunk Mr. C 😲😲😲

GABRIELLE

Sorry - I had phone in pocket LOL

I'm there now ✅ ✅

PRIANKA
ME 2

You don't even know how strong you are.

You are beautiful inside and out!

Love conquers all

Yes we can!

We stand united

CECILY

Guys, I am marrying Mara 2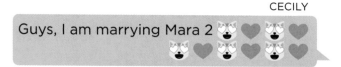

Don't be mad LOL

GABRIELLE

Obv not

That's why marriage booth is so fun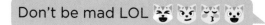

Marry everyone!

PRIANKA

Agree agree

Certificate of Marriage

On this day in
May 2018

Mara Wilder and Cecily Anderson

were joined together in marriage
by the state of
Yorkville Middle School.

Witness: Kelly O.

CECILY

Guys can I just say how glad I am that we talked and r good now & its ok 2 be diff and still be bff 🥀🌷🌷

I am soooo emo rn but ILYSM

GABRIELLE

I am so glad 2

Tolerance comes in many diff ways ya know

PRIANKA

Totes 💯💯💯

We have come sooo far since the V incident

CECILY

🩷 how we r texting about this bc no one can overhear

GABRIELLE

Same 👌👌

We r the best 💗💗💗💗💗💗💗💗💗💗💗💗💗💗💗💗

PRIANKA

Better than best 💃💃💃

GABRIELLE

CPG4eva&eva&eva&eva 🙌 🙌 🙌

YOU ARE
A LOVE
WARRIOR

Spread joy
wherever
you go

Stay strong!
We are all
rooting for
you!

Arjun, Victoria

VICTORIA

r u having fun

ARJUN

I am

Thank u 4 checking

Did u see me on the news last night from when they taped me @ Vish's house a few wks ago

VICTORIA

Noooo were u already on 😲 😩 😲

ARJUN

Yes @ 7pm

VICTORIA

I will have 2 come over and watch 📺 📺

U DVRd it right

Yes

VICTORIA

Ok I am inviting myself over this week

ARJUN

LOL

VICTORIA

Where r u now

Do u want 2 get married

But FYI I've already married 5 peeps

LOL 😂😂

216

From: Mr. Akiyama
To: All Grade Representatives
Subject: Wonderful job!

Dear students,

You all did such an outstanding job with the Spring Fair today. The booths were terrific.

We also raised $1,000 for refugee families settling in Yorkville.

Thank you to everyone, especially the grade reps who put so much work into the booths.

Wonderful work!

#YorkvilleUnited

Mr. Akiyama

 **WE ROCK**

P   C   G

PRIANKA

2day was so fab 👍👍👍👍👍

Cece, sooooo proud of all ur hard work 🏆 💯 💕 💞 🖤 🤍

CECILY

We all did stuff 👧👧👧👧👧

Our whole grade did such a good job 💪💪

& colin's idea 4 the $$ 4 refugee fams was so smart, Gabs 💯💯

GABRIELLE

He is a smart boy 💡💡💡🕺🕺🕺

CECILY

LOL yes 😂😂

PRIANKA

Victoria and Arjun r still going strong ✓ ✓ ✓ 👧 👧

GABRIELLE

That is the funniest part of it all 😂 😂

PRIANKA

Yea true

she doesn't text us as much bc she's always texting him 😳 😪 😨 📱➡️📱

GABRIELLE

Wow hahahaha 😄 😄

CECILY

It's all good tho ✌️ ✌️

I guess things r calm 4 now 💆 💆 💆

PRIANKA

We can always start planning a fall back 2 school kick-off party... 🍃 🍂 🍁 🧜 🎉 💥 🎆 👯

GABRIELLE

LOL can we plz relax & have summer 1st 😎 👙 ☀️ 🕶️ 🏖️ ⛱️ 🤿 🍳 🌅

CECILY

Yesssss 👏 👏 👏 👏 👏 👏

U guys want 2 come over for ice cream sundaes in my backyard 🌲 🌳 🧁 👭 🍨

GABRIELLE

Right now ⛲ ⛲

PRIANKA

????

CECILY

Yesssss why not ❓

PRIANKA

K 👌 💃 🌿 🌷 🍄 🍁 🍂 🐚 🐟 🌵 🍀 🌱 🌿 🌴 🌲 🌲 🍀

GABRIELLE

ON MY WAY 👧 👧 👧 👧

PRIANKA

SAME 😎 🍦 🍨 🤍

CECILY

Hi guys — Pri here. DUHHHH. Funny how we are writing in this notebook even though we are all together right now. But I think we need a real record of our summer together and this is the best way to do it.

Tell me if you agree.

PS: Imagine if our notebook gets published one day like a real book, and then made into a movie, and we become famous...OMG.

I agree! LOVE YOU GUYS! —Cecily Anderson, your BFFFFFFFF

Yes, I agree too!! —Gabrielle Katz

Okay so I'm adding a few more things to the list.

-extra batteries for flashlights

-everyone bring their iPod touch (NO SCREENS LOL)

-extra bug spray

-extra water bottle

-snacks even though it said we aren't supposed to
bring food

-my cute new cutoffs even though it said we
shouldn't bring nice stuff

(LOL I am such a rule breaker :))

-summer reading books

-our journals

-THIS JOURNAL :) :) :)

-digital camera

OMG I AM SOOOOOOO EXCITED!!!!!!!!!!!!!!!!!!

Back to ice cream now?

YES YES YES

DITTO. ILY2SM!!!!!!!

GLOSSARY

2 to

2gether together

4 for

4eva forever

any1 anyone

awk awkward

BFF best friends forever

BFFAE best friends forever and ever

b-room bathroom

b/t between

c see

caf cafeteria

comm committee

comp computer

DEK don't even know

deets details

def definitely

diff different

disc discussion

emo emotional

every1 everyone

fab fabulous

fabolicious extra fabulous

fac faculty

fave favorite

Fla Florida

fone phone

fyi for your information

gtg gotta go

gn good night

gnight good night

gr8 great

hw homework

ICB I can't believe

IDC I don't care

IDEK I don't even know

IDK I don't know

IHNC I have no clue

IK I know

ILY I love you

ILYSM I love you so much

JK just kidding

K okay

L8r later

LMK let me know

lol laugh out loud

luv love

n e way anyway

NM nothing much

nvm never mind

nums numbers

obv obviously

obvi obviously

obvs obviously

OMG oh my God

ooc out of control

peeps people

perf perfect

pgs pages

plzzzz please

pos possibly

q question

r are

ridic ridiculous

rlly really

RN right now

sci science

sec second

sem semester

scheds schedules

some1 someone

SWAK sealed with a kiss

TBH to be honest

thx thanks

TMI too much information

tm tomorrow

tmrw tomorrow

tomrw tomorrow

tomw tomorrow

totes totally

u you

ur your

vv very, very

w/ with

wb write back

w/o without

WIGO what is going on

whatev whatever

wknd weekend

WTH what the heck

wut what

wuzzzz what's

Y why

ACKNOWLEDGMENTS

All my love, appreciation, and gratitude to: Dave, Aleah, Hazel, the Greenwalds, the Rosenbergs, the BWL Library & Tech team, my totes awesome editor, Maria, Rebecca, Katherine, Aurora, Amy, Erica, Bethany, Ann, Stephanie, all the fab peeps at Katherine Tegen Books 👏 👏 💪 💪 👊 , and agent Alyssa. To all of my readers: 😍 😘 2 all of u. ILYSM!

Last but def not least, thanks to Adam, Tatyana, Sammy, Richard, Tobias, Brent, Harris, Carolina, JB, Imara, Lindsay, David, William, Olaf, Paige, Rachel, Olivia, Tiarna, Sam, Julia, Spencer, Harlan, Agatha, Philip, Philip, Cameron, Jack, Hawk, Jenna, Blake, Drew, Robert, Ben, Hudson, Jean-Luc, Charlize, Julian, Sammie, Sasha, Olivia, Ryan, Bijan, Andrew, Ilana, Sophia, Abby, Andrew, Malachi, Hudson, Jack, Lucas, Josh, Jacob, Lissie, Gavin, Gabi, and Emilia for all the help with the text lingo. XOXOXOXOXO ♥ ♥ ♥ ♥ ♥ ♥ ♥ ♥ ♥ ♥ ♥ ♥ ♥

LISA GREENWALD lives in NYC  w/ her husband & 2 young daughters. She ♥s: & . Visit her @ www.lisagreenwald.com.

Don't miss Lisa Greenwald's next book!

Are you ready for more CPG4Eva?
Don't miss *TBH #1: This Is So Awkward* and
TBH #3: Too Much Drama!

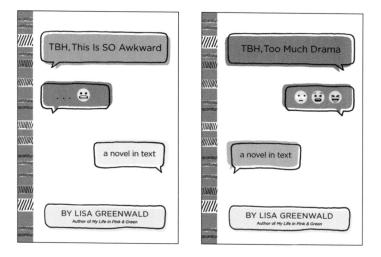